"This book is a special project I created with my daughter, Aahira, when she turned five. Together, we explored the use of Artificial Intelligence. Aahira's imaginative drawings of the characters brought them to life and shaped the story with dramatic twists. Our creative journey turned into this delightful tale, and we hope you enjoy reading it as much as we enjoyed making it.

I am grateful to Maurin for joining us on this delightful journey. Her vibrant and creative illustrations enhance the story, making the reading experience truly magical."

-Abhinav Seth

MIRA's Resolve

Printing in India
ISBN: 978-93-6045-380-0
First Printing, 2024

IndiePress
A division of Nasadiya Technologies Private Ltd. Koramangala, Bengaluru
Karnataka-560029
IndiePress Publications
www.indiepress.in
Edited by Ipsa Seth
Book Cover and Illustrations designed by Maurin Singh
Publishing Consultant - Rechal Fernandes

Mira's Resolve

Story by Abhinav Seth & Aahira Seth

Illustrated by Maurin Singh

In the Valley of Flowers,
alpine blooms bring delight,
buzzing bees work from
morning to night.

"Our world of sweet and bright,
our meadow, blessed by the Almight.
Daughter bee, Mira, take to flight,
join the cheerful, take flight!"

With fellow bees and butterflies,
Mira fluttered, soared in flight.
Jashoda, proud and teary-eyed,
a splendid and wondrous sight.

Iusk deer pranced through the
lade,
heir grace beyond compare,
ray langur in the shade,
heir tails flowed through the air.

eroze, the tortoise,
merged from the Pushwati's embrace.
n this haven of bliss,
ritters, all, found their place.

One dark and cloudy morning
Mira woke with a frown.
No buzzing bees,
no birds with melodic sound.
The flowers, once joyful,
drooped to the ground.

Mira, with concern in her eyes,
searched for her friends, beneath the grey skies.

Worried but determined to unravel the
fate,
Mira, soared to Benny, the butterfly,
asked of their friends in this quiet space.

Benny fluttered her wings and said,
"no buzzing, no cheer,
Mira, we must fear!"

Mira, with her heart full of care,
gathered strength for adventure in the air.

Through the meadow, she roamed, determined to bring her friends back home.

Mira spotted Feroze, his bag set for afar,
he spoke of fading flowers and fruits, a tale bizarre.

Feroze sensed her concern,
under the twilight's evening star.

Before goodbyes, Feroze made his plea,
"Visit Baa, the wise old owl, by the great old tree.
She knows of the world and its secrets so wide,
seek her wisdom," he said with pride.

Mira ventured through the woods,
with a heartfelt prayer and branches everywhere.
Her wings grew tired, the journey was rough,
she rested on a branch and it felt just enough.

She heard an ancient call,
"Mira, my child, you've been seeking m
after all,"
Baa, with wisdom so rare,
knew she needed aid, in the forest so fa

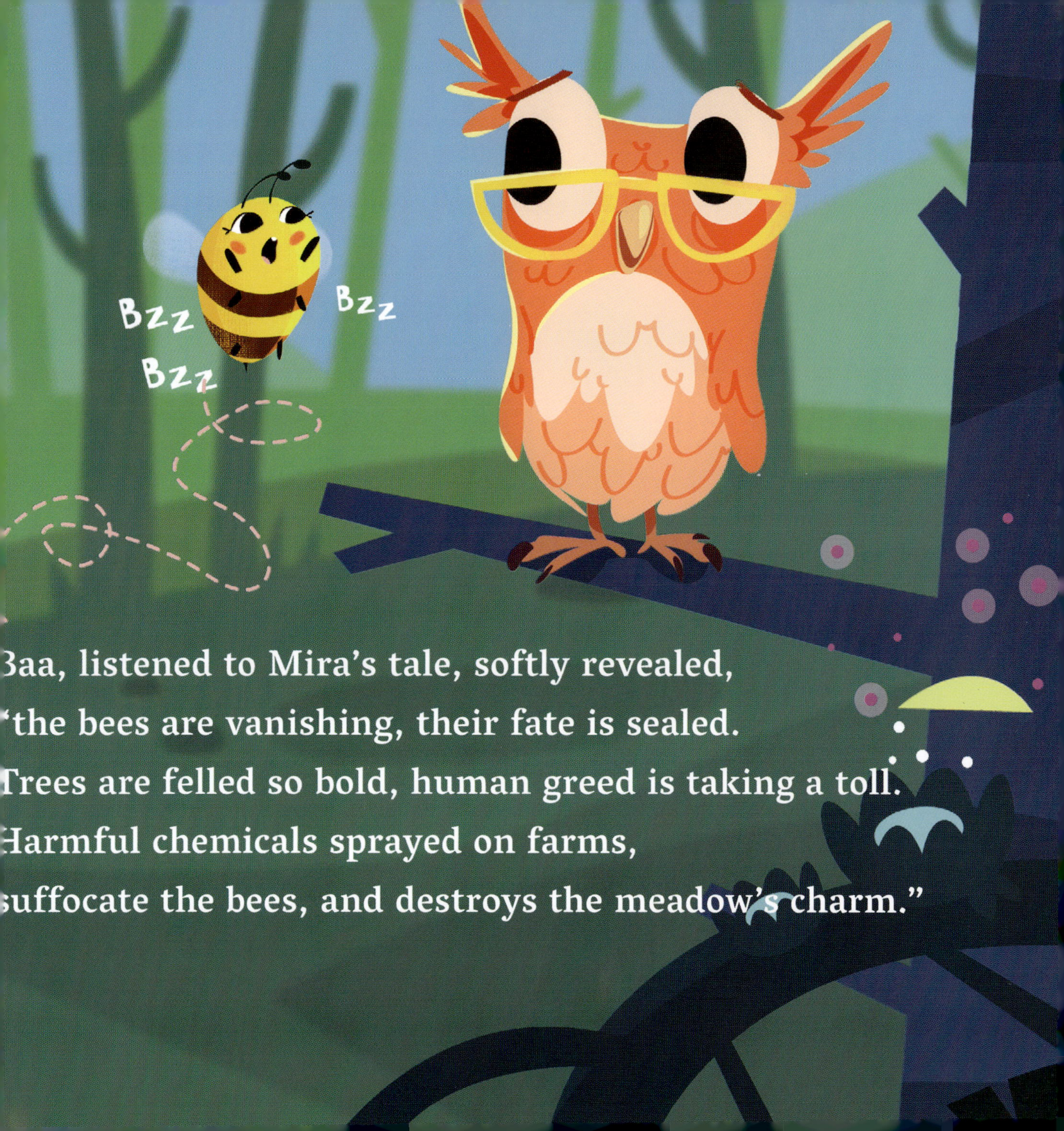

Baa, listened to Mira’s tale, softly revealed,
“the bees are vanishing, their fate is sealed.
Trees are felled so bold, human greed is taking a toll.
Harmful chemicals sprayed on farms,
suffocate the bees, and destroys the meadow’s charm.”

Mira sank deeper in despair,
but her spirits held tight.
Her unwavering faith in the divine,
grew her resolve, a beacon to shine.

She promised to herself,
"I shall help my friends,
and the meadow I adore,
I am committed to protect my home,
where our joy is stored."

A friend of the owl, a fairy named Fay,
overheard Mira's tale as she passed that day.
She offered help to drive the gloom away.

Magic sparkled in the moonlight's gleam.
Mira felt hope, like a wonderful dream.

The night twinkled,
and the tale unfolds.
Mira, propelled by
courage untold.

Mira rallied bees far and near,
spreading the message, crystal clear.
"Save the meadow, save our grace,
tortoise to deer, join the embrace!"

Together they stood, a united parade,
for the meadow they loved, not a bit afraid.

Mira took their plea to the human land,
Fay's magic tuned human hearts to the
sounds of the meadow's band.
"Cease the tree-felling,
end the harmful-spray,
protect the meadow,
let the nature thrive and play."

The humans vowed to preserve the trees and the land,
plant even more, joined in hand in hand.

The meadow transformed, vibrant and aliv
with colours in bloom, fruits revived.
Bees to animals, their hearts cherished,
life danced and flourished.

Mira learned a lesson, profound,
with faith, care, and courage,
the world could be unbound.
Even the tiniest beings,
can bring about a change,
in this vast world,
the life can rearrange.

Remember, young ones, bees are indispensable to us.
We must safeguard them and their habitats to nurture
our planet's health and beauty.
We can contribute by planting flowers and abstaining
from using harmful chemicals in our gardens and farms.

BEE TRIVIA– DO YOU KNOW?

Ques. 1: How long have bees been on our planet?

Answer: Bees have been on our planet for 270 million years before the Dinosaurs!

Ques. 2: How many bees does it take to produce one jar of honey?

Answer: It takes about 25,000 bees to make one jar of honey.

Ques. 3: How far can bees travel collectively to produce one jar of honey?

Answer: Bees can collectively travel over 14,500 kilometers to produce one jar of honey.

Ques. 4: How many species of bees can be domesticated?

Answer: Only two species of bees, the western and eastern honeybees, and their sub-species are domesticated.

Ques. 5: What is the approximate number of bees in a single hive of domesticated honeybee species?

Answer: A single hive of domesticated honeybee species can have up to 60,000 bees.

HELP THE BEE REACH ITS HIVE!